D0872056

Voices
from the
Other World

Voices
from the
Other World

Ancient Egyptian Tales

Naguib Mahfouz

Translated by Raymond Stock

The American University in Cairo Press
Cairo ❧ New York

The American University in Cairo Press
113 Sharia Kasr el Aini, Cairo, Egypt
420 Fifth Avenue, New York, NY 10018
www.aucpress.com

❧ Contents ❧

Chronology of Ancient Egypt   vii

Translator's Introduction   ix

Evil Adored   1

King Userkaf's Forgiveness   13

The Mummy Awakens   27

The Return of Sinuhe   47

A Voice From the Other World   57

Glossary   77

Chronology of Ancient Egypt

Predynastic Period (Neolithic Period–Dynasty 'o')
5500–3050BC
Early Dynastic Period (1st–2nd Dynasties)
3050–2687
Old Kingdom (3rd–6th Dynasties)
2687–2191
First Intermediate Period (7th Dynasty–Early 11th Dynasty)
2191–2061
Middle Kingdom (Late 11th Dynasty–14th Dynasty)
2061–1664
Second Intermediate Period (15th–17th Dynasties)
1664–1569
New Kingdom (18th–20th Dynasties)
1569–1081
Third Intermediate Period (21st–23rd Dynasties)
1081–711
Late Period (24th–31st Dynasties)
724–332
Greco-Roman Period
332BC–395AD

Principal source: Donald B. Redford, editor, *The Oxford Encyclopedia of Ancient Egypt* (Cairo: The American University in Cairo Press, 2001).

❧ Translator's ❧ Introduction

The five little-known stories that make up this volume—drawn from the vast output of Egypt's (and the Arab world's) greatest modern writer—are all in some way inspired by his country's ancient past. Written in the 1930s and 1940s, in the early phase of Naguib Mahfouz's novelistic career—which he began by publishing three books of fiction set in pharaonic times—they may well have been intended as the bases for longer works. Some are in a kind of fable form, as though adapted from folk literature or ancient texts—which, in part, they were. Yet he utterly remade them into his own, and placed them in the cutting-edge literary journals of the day, including three of them ("Evil Adored," "The Mummy Awakens," and "A Voice from the Other World") in his first collection of short stories, *The Whisper of Madness (Hams al-junun*, the date of whose appearance is still debated). The other two—"King Userkaf's Forgiveness" and "The Return of Sinuhe"—have languished in the crumbling pages of aging magazines, uncollected and largely ignored.

Critics have occasionally discussed the stories (with the apparent exception of "Sinuhe"), yet they remained untranslated (but for "The Mummy Awakens," published in English in Pakistan in 1986[1])—and so they moldered unknown to those whose who do not read Arabic. That is, until now, when, like Sinuhe himself, and the born-again warrior unhappy with the changes since antiquity in Mahfouz's mummy adventure, they have come back to remind us of our more than half-century neglect of their undeniable charms.

In his pharaonic stories as in his others, Mahfouz combines historical observation with a timeless imagination. The story here with the least direct connection to any known events or legends is the first one, "Evil Adored." Set in still little-understood Predynastic Egypt, after the first few sentences—which explain that the country had at one time been divided into autonomous districts—it bears little resemblance to any confirmed ancient source or reality. Yet this hardly diminishes its allegorical appeal.

Likewise, the second tale, "King Userkaf's Forgiveness," while featuring the true founder of the Fifth Dynasty as its title character, and liberally marbled with allusions to real places and people (including Userkaf's son and successor, Sahura), is not based upon any known incident. Indeed, the real Userkaf's scarcely-documented reign (2513–2506 BC) offered a nearly clean slate for Mahfouz's fictional agenda. An avid reader of ancient Egyptian literature, Mahfouz may well have taken Userkaf's final state of mind from *The Teaching of Amenemhat*, a renowned poem from Egypt's Middle Kingdom. In this poem, Amenemhat I, founder of the Twelfth Dynasty (r. 1991–1962 BC), appears in a dream—after his assassination in an intrigue hatched by his chief vizier and women from his

---

1 Roger Allen, "The Mummy Awakes," *The Worlds of Muslim Imagination*, ed. Algamir Hashmi (Islamabad: Gulhomar, 1986), pp. 15–33, commentary pp. 212–15.

harem—to his son, Senwosret I, confirming his succession to the throne. Amenemhat sadly warns (as translated by Richard B. Parkinson): "Trust no brother! Know no friend! Make for yourself no intimates—this is of no avail!"

The next story, "The Mummy Awakens," is perhaps the only one that Mahfouz has published that features an outright political tirade—though delivered in the 1930s by a mummy from the Eighteenth Dynasty. A tongue-in-cheek adaptation of the standard plots of Hollywood mummy movies then in vogue (as they are again today), the mummy's character is perhaps loosely based on Horemheb, the general who served under the "heretic king" Akhenaten (r. ca. 1372–1355 BC), who later become pharaoh himself (r. 1343–1315 BC).

Further testifying to Mahfouz's lifelong fascination with the literary heritage of the pharaonic age, the fourth story is fashioned in part from a classic Egyptian text, *The Tale of Sinuhe.* In "The Return of Sinuhe," Mahfouz includes many of the ancient story's elements—but adds a crucial one only vaguely implied in the Middle Kingdom original: the romance. Parkinson, one of *The Tale of Sinuhe*'s most famous translators[2] and a renowned expert on ancient Egyptian literature overall, calls the nearly four-thousand-year-old poem "a fictional work of the highest artistry." He is equally enamored of Mahfouz's version—which Parkinson has hailed as "wonderful."

The fifth and final story offers an appropriately spiritual exit from Mahfouz's ancient Egyptian universe. "A Voice from the Other World" astoundingly anticipates, by at least three decades, the popular wave of 'out-of-body experience' literature that swept

2 Richard B. Parkinson, *The Tale of Sinuhe and other Ancient Egyptian Poems, 1940–1640 BC* (Oxford University Press, 1997).

the publishing world in the 1970s and 1980s. Yet it is almost certainly set in the time of Ramesses II (r. 1304–1227 BC), as the story's protagonist appears loosely modeled on Pentaweret (Pentu-wer)—once thought to have composed the epic poem that he inscribed on this king's monuments trumpeting the (much-disputed) triumph over the Hittite forces at Qadesh. Likewise, the other period details are for the most part plausible. These include Mahfouz's description of the tomb and its contents, his reference to the feast of Isis, plus his repeated use of the ancient (and still extant) Egyptian identification of the West—the land of the sunset—as the abode of Death. And, with one or two minor exceptions, Mahfouz renders the methods of mummification employed in the New Kingdom with gruesome precision. Even more importantly, however, he creates a truly vivid glimpse into that other existence after this one—and his vision is sanguine.

And so this quintet of vintage tales has been saved from the near oblivion that for many years had claimed them. The same fate had befallen his three early pharaonic novels, as well: *'Abath al-aqdar* (*Khufu's Wisdom*, 1939); *Radubis* (*Rhadopis*, 1943), and *Kifah Tiba* (*Thebes at War*, 1944). They had been overshadowed by his splendid *Trilogy* (*Palace Walk, Palace of Desire*, and *Sugar Street*) and other works set in modern Cairo and Alexandria. But no more. Thanks to the American University in Cairo Press, which brought out his brilliant 1985 novella *al-'A'ish fi-l-haqiqa*, set in ancient Egypt, under the title *Akhenaten: Dweller in Truth* (translated by Tagried Abu-Hassabo), in 1998, these forgotten historical gems will soon make their debut in English. (They began to appear in Europe, principally in French, Italian, and Spanish, in the 1990s.)

Together with this book, they launch a much-deserved introduction of some of the master's finest (but most unusual, and least familiar) works to readers of English. Like their ninety-one-year-old author, their spirits, for all their wisdom, remain forever young—though they speak with voices from a world much different from the one for which he is best known.

The translator thanks Roger Allen, Kathleen Anderson, Hazem Azmy, Brooke Comer, Gaballa Ali Gaballa, Zahi Hawass, Prince Abbas Hilmi, Shirley Johnston, Klaus Peter Kuhlmann, Mark Linz, Bojana Mojsov, Richard B. Parkinson, Donald Malcolm Reid, Veronica Rodriguez, Rainer Stadelmann, Helen Stock, Paul Theroux, Peter Theroux, and David Wilmsen for their helpful comments on the present work, as well as Kelly Zaug and R. Neil Hewison for their excellent editing. And, above all, he thanks Naguib Mahfouz—for patiently, as always, answering endless questions about these stories.

Evil Adored

Before the first king ruled on the throne of Egypt, the great valley of the Nile was divided into independent districts, each with its own god, religion, and sovereign. One of these nomes, called Khnum, was famed for its fertile soil, favorable climate, and plentiful population. Yet its fate was cruelly wrought by hardships and woes, for while the opulent lived in sin, the peasants went without food. As the wicked dwelt on the land in wanton corruption, disease and pestilence claimed the wretched and the weak. The men in charge of the district—chief amongst them the magistrate Sumer, the constable Ram, and the physician Toheb—set to work on reform. Their fierce campaign to suppress crime and depravity became the model far and wide for righteousness, integrity, and moral resolve.

During one of the generations that passed in this district, there came a stranger—an elderly gentleman, clean-shaven on both his head and his face (as was the custom for Egyptian priests), tall and gauntly built. His gaze bore a sharp expression, mocking his advanced age, radiating the light of intelligence and wisdom. He truly was peculiar, for no sooner would he set foot in a land then its people would begin to ask in amazement, "Who is this man? . . .

What country drove him out? . . . What does he want? . . . And how does he roam the earth at a time when he really should rest in pious peace of mind while awaiting his crossing to the world of Osiris?"

His eccentric character knew no bounds. He left behind him a vortex of disorder and a whorl of uproar wherever he settled down—and wherever he headed. He prowled the markets and the temples, inviting himself to parties without knowing their hosts, injecting himself into what did not concern him. He would talk to husbands about their wives and to wives about their husbands, to fathers about their sons and to sons about their fathers, engaging in argument with the lords and the nobles. He also spoke with the servants and the slaves, leaving in his wake a deep and powerful influence that stirred defiant revolt in their souls, around which disputation and mutual hostility grew ever stronger.

The stranger's way of life aroused the fears of Ram, the protector of order. He followed him around like his shadow, observing him closely, filled with suspicion about his intentions. At length he seized him and led him to the magistrate, so that he could examine his astounding case. Sumer the magistrate was a man of advanced years and vast experience: he had spent four decades of his magnificent life in heroic struggle under the banners of Truth and Justice. He had personally dispatched hundreds of rebels to their proper fate, and filled the prisons with thousands of evildoers and criminals, as he labored faithfully and sincerely to cleanse the district of the enemies of peace and tranquility.

But when this odd man came before him, Sumer felt astonished and confused. He wondered to himself what this used-up old coot could have done—then, casting an appraising glance upon him, he asked in his weighty voice, "What, venerable sir, is your name?"

The man did not answer. Instead, he remained silent, shaking

his head as though he did not wish to speak—or did not know what
to say.

The judge, annoyed by his unreasonable silence, demanded in a
harsh voice, "Why don't you answer? State your name!"

The man replied in a murmur, a faint, ambiguous smile upon his
lips, "I do not know, sire."

The magistrate's anger redoubled, and he demanded scoldingly,
"Do you really not know your name?"

"Yes, sire—I have forgotten it."

"Do you really claim that you have forgotten your own name—the
name that people call you?"

"No one uses any name for me: my family and close friends have all
passed away. I have wandered in this world for a very long time, but no
one addresses me by name. No human being calls out to me, and—with
my head overflowing with ideas and dreams—I have forgotten it."

Sumer berated the old man for his feebleminded senility—then
turned away from him in despair to the protector of order. He asked,
"What drove you to bring this man to my courtroom?"

"He is, sire," said Ram, "a man who neither rests nor permits others to rest. He imposes himself upon people and makes them debate
both good and evil—and does not bid them farewell until dissension
and division have rent them apart."

The magistrate tilted toward Ram and inquired, "What does he
want, behind all that?"

The old man fixed a sharp look upon him. In a voice strong in tone
but quavering from the many years that he had dwelt in this life, he
replied, "I want to reform this beastly world, my lord."

The judge smiled and asked him, "Do we not find those who give
their lives unstintingly to this noble work when they can? What does
the judge, the police chief, or the doctor do? Be reassured, old man,

and put yourself at ease, for your great age cannot shoulder this grueling task—there are others more capable than yourself."

The man shook his head stubbornly and said, "All those that you have cited have been around since the beginning of creation. Yet they have not yet been able to alter this brutality that so disfigures the world. We still see, in every corner of the earth, the harbingers of evil and the plain signs of crime."

"And are you succeeding, then, even as all these amassed forces have failed?"

"Indeed, sire . . . bear with me, and I will show you."

Amused, the magistrate smiled again, then asked, "And what means do you possess that they do not?"

"My lord, they drive out wrongdoers, treat the sick, and bind up the wounded. But as for me, my method is to eliminate the malady entirely. Disease is a sneak attack on the refuge of our well-being. Those others care only about its symptoms. I have examined this very carefully, and discovered that the stomach is the basis of the malaise in this region. I found many that could not fill its gaping emptiness, so that they howl from hunger. At the same time, others are not only not empty, but consume greedily all that they wish. And from the mutual attraction and revulsion of these two stomachs comes looting, pillage, and murder. So the disease is clear—and the treatment is clear, as well."

The judge rejoined, "To the contrary: the disease that you have diagnosed has no cure!"

"That is what they say, sire. And they say this only because because they lack something crucial to Our Lord: that is, faith in Him, the belief in Virtue. They do not have the proper faith in goodness. They struggle for its sake using passive tools that have no feeling, and labor for wages, status, and glory. And if they retreat unto themselves, worn out by what they declare to be their disgust with sinfulness, then that is their business, sire. As for myself, I believe properly in Virtue—which bids me to proceed down my path, and to do so slowly and gently."

The man's speech stirred anger in the constable's soul, the more so as he seemed to be slandering him right in his presence. But the magistrate, being more broadminded and softhearted, showed forebearance to what the man said. Not finding anything in his actions that warranted punishment, Sumer released him with a word of caution.

The man left the courtroom, charged with the elation of youth. The approval on high for his mission seemed even more certain, as he stalked the earth with the strength of a giant, gushing forth in speech with the zeal of a youngster, his heart bursting with the optimism of a prophet. His tongue spat out a kind of white magic—a way of reasoning that even the haughty could not resist. In a brief time he was able to monopolize the ears of the tribe, to enchant their hearts, arouse their charitable feelings, and to point them in whatever direction he wished. The poor flocked to him, the rich deferred to him; the rebel and the subversive submitted to him. The basis of his appeal was Beauty and Moderation, in whose shade the poor could live in contentment, and the rich would feel that they have enough to be satisfied. In him, this sick society found a sound and skillful physician—and so they clung to his example, embracing his ideals.

The results were breathtaking, dazzling the seers and the wise men alike. They wiped out crime, put evil to flight, and remedied all ills. The spreading wings of happiness sheltered the district. The civic leaders rejoiced, praising and putting their faith in the man whom they had previously disbelieved. They reveled at finally reaching the noble end that they had spent their whole lives trying vainly to achieve.

Time marched on, smoothly and quietly, in an atmosphere of calm—as things changed into a state that people had never before seen. The authorities were the first to feel the coming of the new age. In truth, they found themselves with nothing to do—and leisure delights only those who work for a living. The empty hours grew heavier and heavier upon them—as, with mournful eyes, they watched their majesty fade, their wind blow away, and their radiance dim into gloom.

In the past, the constable had the power to spread panic wherever he paused for an instant. But now he had become a thing that people looked back at defiantly, with blatant contempt—to the point where they trod blithely past him as they would a broken idol.

And the magistrate, who had wielded his sacred power with a divine dignity, was now sheepish with anguish and sorrow. He heard not a greeting nor an urgent request, nor did he return the welcome of those who called out to him. He felt only loneliness and isolation, until he became like an abandoned temple in the desert.

As for the doctor, groaning from hidden complaints, he locked himself in his house—neither receiving guests, nor visiting anyone else. Before this, he had hoarded money in a cooking pot, but now he had started to use up what he had saved, while his heart pounded with worry.

Meanwhile, the province rested secure in its state of grace—except for those who had deluded themselves into believing that they were the 'Manufacturers of Virtue.' They were now desperate and perplexed, turning left and right for a way out of this distressing situation. Yet they could find none. The constable suffered most of all, because—though the boldest among them—he nonetheless dreaded declaring his anxieties, only to encounter deaf ears and confident, contented hearts.

Finally, his patience exhausted, he seized the opportunity offered by a meeting with his peers to wonder aloud, in a voice filled with fear, "What would we do if the Sovereign—as of tomorrow—should have no more need of our services?"

Their faces went blank. Stammering, one of them asked, "Is it likely that he could really do without us?"

Ram said, shrugging his shoulders in disdain, "What can we do to merit being kept on?"

With these words, it was as if he had lifted the lid from an overfilled kettle, and all inside it came spilling out. One of them said, "You cannot keep quiet in a fix like this."

Shaking his fist, another shouted, "That doting old man has ruined the district!"

A third complained, "He is wrecking the human capacity for loftiness with this corrupting appeal, that hinders all progress and slaughters all fears."

The secret talk stirred among them, as each revealed what was inside him— except for the magistrate. He stuck to his silence, gazing off into the distant horizons as though he heard nothing of what was being said around him. His apparition nearly caused many of them to give up hoping for his aid, until Ram whispered to them in embarrassment, "Don't worry about Sumer—his heart is with us. It's just that his tongue, which is used to speaking about Justice, will not obey him in pursuing our purpose here."

And so they all agreed about what to do . . . .

One morning, the sun rose to reveal that the alien man had vanished. His disciples searched for him everywhere, ransacking every corner of the nome—without finding a single trace.

His disappearance came as a confounding surprise—and it provoked differing remarks. Some said that he had moved out of the district after making sure that his creed had been firmly rooted there. Others claimed that he had ascended into heaven after carrying out his mission. Regardless, sadness enfolded the entire province, and all those within it.

Except for those in powerful positions. They let out their breath, and—with hopes high—they each dreamed of their glory that had fled, their comfort that had disappeared. Filled with anticipation, they waited expectantly for these things to return.

But disappointment awaits whoever puts his faith in such expectant hope. When the big shots saw that the ordinary people still clung to their belief—true in their remembrance of the aged outsider—they were struck with disquiet. Their hearts were vexed, and they could not sleep.

Fuming with rage, the protector of order cried, "This situation cannot stand!"

Eyes filled with longing looked toward him. The hard work of hoping had drained them. Perceiving this, Ram said in a conspiratorial tone, "In the province of Ptah, I know of an enticing dancer, to whom the gods have given irresistible beauty. Why don't we borrow her for a few months? I am aware that the ruler of that district is anxious to get rid of her, because her looks are inciting strife and turmoil there. Let the nome of Khnum be her place of exile for a while, and she will no doubt sow divisions between brother and brother, and between husband and wife. The affluent will be agitated to burst the chains that they have put obediently around their own necks. Keep a lookout for a good result soon. "

And so this inspired man put into action his dangerous plan.

With joyous, gleaming eyes, they all witnessed the edifice of the old stranger's regime break down and fall apart, stone by stone. The stomach returned to its throne, commanding necks and minds alike to bend to its rule. The devilish life came back to quiet Khnum, blowing away the serenity that had prevailed in its parts. The gang of leading citizens resumed their campaign, finding themselves once again fighting the good fight—for Virtue, Justice, and Peace.

King Userkaf's Forgiveness

Pharaoh Userkaf was among the most magnificent monarchs of the Fifth Dynasty, who ruled Egypt by blending justice with mercy, firmness with sagacity, and force with affection. When he first took the throne, he mustered a mighty army to march into the Western Desert. His purpose was to squelch the impudence of the wandering tribes—whom his forebears had wooed to make peace—in preying on caravans, pillaging the Delta villages, and attacking peaceful citizens. He crushed them so utterly that his army came back heavily laden with both prisoners and their herds. In this way, he bolstered his own authority—making it, and the name of Egypt—things to be feared, while saving his country's people from the savage tribes' evil. In the shade of peace and security, he devoted all of his care to the domestic affairs of the nation and the welfare of her children. He cut out roads and dug canals, and built for himself a great pyramid at Aswan, his royal capital. His reign was one of safety, wealth, and construction, and the king dwelt, content and confident, among his glorious subjects. His breast was gladdened by his people's love for their king, and his days and nights were brightened by the sincerity of a band of his highest subordinates in their consuming fondness for him. They were his most excellent friends and most splendid companions: his son Sahura, the heir apparent, and Horurra, his chief vizier. There was also Samun, high priest of the god Khnum, as well as Samunra, supreme commander of the Egyptian army.

It was among the customs of the upright king to pray each morning in the Temple of Khnum. On one of these mornings, he entered the Holy of Holies and secluded himself with the deity's statue. He kissed its foot, then prayed fervently in profound gratitude, enumerating his many gifts and blessings. He ended his prayer by saying: "Praise be to my father Khnum for having invested me with people's love and genuine loyalty, for the love of that which he has created is the Creator's satisfaction. There is no one happier in the world than one who brightens the hearts of others for the sake of his own happiness, and who suffers for their suffering."

Because the people of those days worshiped the gods with hearts filled with honesty, faith, and naiveté, the deities would grace them with speech sometimes, and with miracles at others. And so it was not strange for Pharaoh to hear a heavenly voice answer him:

"I granted you wisdom, O King—so why do you place so much confidence in others?"

The king was astonished at what the god had said. Distress rising in his heart, he replied with devout humility, "O Sacred Lord, I have served my people sincerely, and they have given me their love. I have been loyal to my friends, and they are bound in loyalty to me. How could this be a cause for reproach?"

The celestial voice, exalted beyond all equal or description, answered him:

"Behold the tree rich with leaves, whose branches covered in luxuriant greenery fill up the air. See how the people take refuge in its spreading shade from the burning rays of the sun, and how they pluck its low-hanging fruit.

*Then look upon this same tree in winter. See how the cold winds have
stripped it bare, and how all of its leaves have fallen, and how its limbs are
empty and exposed like a decaying corpse which embalming has not pre-
served. See then how the people forsake it, cutting off its branches to throw
them in the fire."*

Pharaoh returned to his palace, depressed and dejected, ponder-
ing over and over again the meaning of what the god had told him.
Doubt whispered in his breast and worry ruled his heart. For the first
time, he began to envision the dear faces that accompanied him over
so many long years in friendship and serenity with an aura of suspicion. He detected behind their amiable chatter naught but honey-
coated lies, beyond their smiles only disgusting hypocrisy, and in their
shows of obedience but the marks of dread and fear. A wave of vio-
lent, malevolent thought washed over him, and he wanted to return
to that happy, vanished past whose white pages were now sullied with
vile imaginings. It appeared to him that his life, which he had once
felt securely to be an unbroken chain of joys, had been spurned by the
eye of Fate . . . a revolting farce and miserable misfortune hidden by
a mask of fraudulent bliss.

Prince Sahura observed the king's strange condition. Confused
and discomfited, he asked his father what was troubling his tranquility. The prince loved his father to the point of worship, and the king
loved his son as the most precious thing in his world. He trusted him
as he trusted himself, so he confided in him the cause of his sorrow.
He told him of his fears, and apprised him of his conversation with
the god Khnum. Embarrassed, the prince did not know how to ban-
ish the phantoms of suspicion from Pharaoh's mind.

Instead, the king continued to dwell on these thoughts, and said
to his intended successor, "I cannot make an example of the deceivers
without tangible proof of their duplicity. But I have arrived at a

means by which I might expose their secret selves. So listen to me, my son: Starting tomorrow, I shall undertake a journey to the land of Punt. During my absence, you shall be charged with care of the State. Wait some days, then declare yourself sovereign over the Valley of the Nile. Entice my closest associates with high position and money. Make them promises and be generous with them—so that they lower their shield of submissiveness and obedience. By this means, we may see what is truly inside them."

But the prince's heart recoiled from Pharaoh's plan. He remonstrated, saying, "I beg you, my lord, not to persuade me to take a position by which my youthful rebellion will be known to both heaven and earth! Nor to accept your long absence, which would rob my heart of its peace, and deprive the people of your care and watchfulness."

But the king prevailed over the prince's anxieties, convincing him to bow to his wishes out of a sense of subservience. Userkaf then went to the youthful Queen Tey—she was not the heir apparent's mother, who had died a long time before—to bid her goodbye. He also bid goodbye to his dear dog, Zay. Then he set out on a merchant ship to the sacred land of Punt, the source of fragrant incense. There he dwelt for not a little while, wandering among her lush, fertile valleys. Everywhere that he set down his foot, he received the honor and hospitality befitting one of Pharaoh's subjects.

Yet Userkaf could not cease thinking about what he might encounter from his subjects and his companions upon his return. Whenever ill-thought tormented him, and deadly dreams and apprehensions appeared to him, he sought relief in beautiful memories, to evoke the feeling of trust they had given him, and to seek patience and repose from their inspiration. And when his breast was weighed down by worry and evil whisperings, and his heart stricken by homesickness, he longed to return to his native land.

So he gathered his scant baggage and sailed on an Egyptian ship, stepping once more onto the shore of that country to which he had offered the flower of his life for the sake of her welfare. He headed straight from the dock to the nearest village, where—dressed as a foreigner—he mixed, unrecognized, among its people. One day he asked a group of them, "O you men, who is your king?"

A young man with a sunburned face answered him, twirling an axe in his arms, "The blessed one's name is Sahura.'"

"And how do you see him?"

The young man answered with a passion to which his friends said, "Amen":

"He comes to our aid if the Nile is too low, and helps us if calamity worsens, and all turns to gloom."

The king then asked, "And how do you remember Userkaf?"

"Well enough—if he were still on the scene, and he were still our king."

Pharaoh sighed, and asked in a wistful voice, "How can you abandon him, when he had been for you a most laudable ruler and guide?"

The youth threw him a nasty look, then said, as he gave him his back, "Sedition is an evil cursed by the gods."

The king left the village in a melancholy way, heading toward the Nile and the seat of his realm. Looking up, he found himself facing the Temple of Khnum. He asked to meet Samun, the high priest, and was invited to enter the inner sanctum. When the high priest saw him, he knew him despite his alien attire. Overwhelmed with amazement and anguish, he shouted out hoarsely, "My lord, King Userkaf!"

The king smiled a bitter, sardonic smile, "How can you call me your lord the king when you have given your blessing to a childish usurper who has stolen my throne?"

The high priest stammered, trembling and looking away, "My lord, what can a weak man do who is not used to fighting?"

"Fighting is not a duty to which all men are bound, but loyalty is incumbent upon all men of virtue. So how can you continue in service to one who has betrayed your lord and benefactor?"

The embarrassment of the king's old friend increased and perplexity gripped him; he did not answer. So Pharaoh said to him, "Are you able, Samun, to repent for your sin by declaring the illegality of my son Sahura's rule, and to offer a service that, by its execution, would encourage me to restore my trust in you of old?"

But the high priest was horrified, and implored him, "I cannot, my lord . . . My duty is to serve my God, not to bring down kings."

Userkaf fell silent for a moment, following with his two stern eyes the eyes of the priest, which avoided his own. Then the king turned his back on him abruptly, and left the temple, sick in his soul, his chest tightening, while he gnawed at his fingers in grief and chagrin.

He proceeded hurriedly to the palace of the vizier Horurra, demanding permission to see him. But the servants mocked his wretched appearance, and started to throw him out. He begged and pleaded with them, but this only made them more arrogant. He then told them that he was a friend of the minister's, and mentioned a name that proved his intimacy—so they let him inside. When the vizier's gaze fell on the man coming toward him, he stood stiff with fright, his limbs frozen and his eyes open wide, and he gasped without thinking, "My lord!"

"May the God treat you kindly, my dear friend, Horurra," said the king.

"Did anyone see you enter my house?" the vizier asked, his heart dismayed.

The king pondered the reason behind this question, and said, beginning to sink into woe and despair, "Yes, my friend—the servants and the guards who gather at your door."

"Did any one of them recognize you?"

"I know not," the king replied.

The vizier sighed, "What a calamity if the King knew of your visit to my house."

"Do you fear this upstart?"

"How could I not?" said the vizier. "You had best leave my palace by the back door."

"My dear friend, Horurra—are you turning me away?"

"Please forgive me, but I'm in difficult straits—I implore you in the name of our old friendship."

Pharaoh laughed derisively, seeing his chief minister in an anxious state that he could only bewail. He saw that hope was useless, and that there was no choice but to quit the palace from the rear entrance, as his friend had wished. So he did depart, as the anguish and regret welled up within his breast.

Of all his friends, none remained but General Samunra. Despite all the failure he had just experienced, the king's bitter forebodings did not vanquish his unshakeable confidence in his commander-in-chief, who was a gallant, noble, and utterly earnest man. The gods had singled him out with a nature that neither treachery nor worldly goods could seduce. So, placing his last hopes upon him, Userkaf asked for permission to go in to see him. When his eyes fell upon him, the king's heart yearned for him and he called out, opening his arms wide to embrace him, "O General Samunra, don't you remember me?"

Flabbergasted, the commander stood up in alarm saying, "My lord, King Userkaf!"

"Yes, it is he himself, in all his misery and remorse."

The general did not see the king's open arms, while his face showed the signs of hardness and severity. He asked his former suzerain sternly, "Does his Majesty the King know of your entering his kingdom?"

Userkaf was taken aback; his arms dropped in deep disappointment.

"No," he said tersely.

"What did you come to do in Egypt?"

"I came to call out for help to my old friends."

The general approached the king, saying in a military voice, "My duty as commander of the Egyptian Army requires that I arrest you in the name of Pharaoh."

"Do you not realize that I am the legitimate king?"

The general said, as he laid his hand upon Userkaf's shoulder, "Egypt has only one king: I know no other."

Convinced that argument was futile, Pharaoh surrendered himself to Samunra. He followed him to the royal palace, where the commander entered the great hall of the throne, halting before the king. Userkaf looked upon his son seated in his own place, around him his own men of state. At their head were Horurra and Samun: he knew that these two had gone straight to Sahura together to tell of his own appearance. And within himself he lauded the two of them coming to give witness. With them, the general would testify to Userkaf's return to the throne, pledging him the loyalty entrusted to the faithful hands of his son. Together they had tasted the shame and disgrace that had tortured their wicked souls—and now were driven to repentance.

The king gazed at his son with a meaningful smile. But just as he was about to speak, he heard a dog's loud barking. He saw Zay cutting through the ranks of the guards, rushing up to him with irresistible force. Pharaoh stroked him with his hands, treating him with a deep concern that bespoke his ardent love and yearning. At the same time, he was not able to control his rage or to calm his mind except with a mighty effort. Then—yielding at last to his fury—he strode firmly up to the throne until he stood before the guards. He looked upon his son with consternation, saying, "Rise, my son, for my experiment is finished. Invite me to appear before these hypocrites." But his son did not rise, nor vacate his place for him. Instead, he said to him, with the majesty of authority, "What have you come to do here? You—the man to whom the gods gave a vast kingdom—but who disdained his right, and went to dally in the land of Punt?"

The son's speech settled on his father like a sentence. His eyes widened and his amazement grew to madness; his stupefied face kept turning back and forth between his haughty son and his gloating men. Losing his tolerance, Sahura burst out cruelly.

"I am now entitled to sever your head from your body. But I have not forgotten that you are my father. I would prefer to avoid this crime that our traditions condemn. Therefore—having opened my breast for you patiently—I grant you a day to prepare yourself. You will then go to the land of Nubia. "

His retinue extolled the charitable act of the king, their tongues ceaselessly showering him with prayers of praise. As for Userkaf, his sense of tribulation intensified until his own tongue was tied and his limbs were paralyzed. Meanwhile, his dog Zay sensed his pain; he kept on barking and tugging on his cloak that was covered with dust from his wanderings.

The king then roused himself against his weakness, and spoke to his son. "And Queen Tey?"

"She is now the queen of contented Egypt."

The king sighed and asked, "May I be so bold as to ask that Zay might accompany me?"

"That I grant you—his barking annoys us."

So the king left the land of Egypt in guilt and sadness, humiliated by his misfortune. As he headed into exile, his faithful dog followed him. He arrived in the land of Nubia, where he lived among its mountains in fearful isolation, speaking to no one. But as his cares and angst pressed down upon him, the solitary creature that showed him love and devotion, bearing the pangs of deprivation patiently for his sake, gave voice to his complaints.

The governor of Nubia did not leave him alone for long. He visited him and invited him to visit as well, withholding from him neither warmth nor welcome. He wasted no time in revealing his hidden self. Userkaf found him a grumbler who saw his station in Nubia as an offense against his person, which showed a lack of appreciation for his services and qualifications. And therefrom glimmered in the heart of the king a gleam of hope. He exploited the governor's discontent, indulging his delusions, until the disgruntled man consented to dispatch Nubian and Egyptian troops northward, with Pharaoh at their lead. Sahura readied his own army to rebuke them: the two armies met in a decisive battle—in which Userkaf triumphed. He entered his capital as a conquering king, arrested his son and his friends of yore, and threw them into the dungeon.

When Queen Tey learned of the victory of her former husband's army she succumbed to terror, and took her own life—thus robbing Userkaf of the opportunity to avenge himself upon her. But, in reality, the king was not ready to make any decisions, nor to decree the fate of any of his prisoners until his anger had cooled and the intoxication of his victory had subsided. He took the time to review, to contemplate, and to consider. He stayed up a long evening thinking and reflecting, until, finally, he was guided to an opinion.

In the morning, he commanded his son and his companions to come to him upon his throne. They all prostrated themselves, avert-

24

ing their glances, debased and vanquished by their own obsequiousness. The king regarded them for a long time, an ambiguous smile upon his lips. Then he addressed them, with a shocking serenity.

"I have forgiven you—all of you."

Bafflement swept over them—they could not believe their ears. They stared in awe at the king seated upon his throne, exchanging looks of confounded incredulity. Pharaoh spoke to them again in his wondrous calm, "I know what I am saying—I have indeed pardoned you all. Return to your posts and direct yourselves to your tasks with the purpose and sincerity with which I have charged you."

The governor of Nubia was unable to restrain himself, saying, "You would pardon, my lord, those who usurped your throne, and drove you from your kingdom without mercy? You would forgive them, my lord, whose robes are still splotched with the blood of those that they slew in fighting you?"

The king said, still smiling, "Who would be my new heir apparent? And who would be a more pious priest than Samun, or a more able vizier than Horurra, or a more skillful commander than Samunra? If only Queen Tey had not hastened to put an end to herself—for I would love that she were seated next to me on this throne once more. As for sincerity, my dear governor, I have come to the point of thinking the worst of all men. I hold no more trust in you than in these others—for all people seek refuge in the shade of the leafy tree, but when winter strips it bare they forsake it without regret. Therefore it would gain me nothing to put these people to death. On the contrary—for I would find no one better to take their places."

And so King Userkaf lived the rest of his life at an emotional remove from the world. He knew no intimates in his palace at Aswan—not from the teeming masses of his people, nor from his covetous royal courtiers. There was only his loyal friend, Zay.

The Mummy
Awakens

I am deeply embarrassed to tell this tale—for some of its events violate the laws of reason and of nature altogether. If this were merely fiction, then it would not cause me to feel such embarrassment. Yet it happened in the realm of reality—and its victim was one of the most renowned and extraordinary men of Egypt's political and aristocratic circles. Moreover, I am relating it as recorded by a great professor in the national university. There is no room for doubt of his sentience or his character, nor is he known for any tendency toward delusions or wild stories. Still, it may truly be said, I do not know how to believe it myself, nor to persuade others to do so. This is not due to the want of miracles and wonders in our time. Yet rational people of our day do not accept matters without good cause—just as they do not oppose putting faith in something if there is a logical explanation for it. Though the strange account that I now transmit has claims of authenticity, a coherent narrative, and tangible attestations, the scientific basis for it is still much in doubt. Would I not, then, express my hesitation in presenting it?

Whatever one makes of the matter, here it is as portrayed by Dr. Dorian, professor of Ancient Egyptian Archaeology at Fuad I University:

On that painful day, when the heart of Egypt shook with anguish and sorrow, I went to visit the late Mahmoud Pasha al-Arna'uti at his grand country palace in Upper Egypt. I remember that I found the Pasha with a group of friends that flocked around him when circumstances permitted. Among them was M. Saroux, headmaster at the school of fine arts, and Dr. Pierre, the expert on mental diseases. We all gathered in his elegant, sophisticated salon, filled with the choicest examples of contemporary art—both paintings and sculpture. It was as though they were marshaled in that place in order to convey the salute of the genius of modernity to the memory of the immortal Pharaonic spark. Buried in the ruins of the Nile Valley, its light nonetheless burned through the darkness of the years like the points of the harmonious stars in the sky, a voyager through the void of the jet-black night.

The deceased was among the richest, most cultured people in Egypt, and the noblest in disposition. His friend Professor Lampere once said of him that he was "three persons in one"—for he was Turkish in race, Egyptian in nationality, and French in his heart and mind. To achieve his acquaintance was the height of accomplishment.

In fact, the Pasha was France's greatest friend in the East—he thought of her as his second country. His happiest days were those that he spent beneath her skies. All of his companions were drawn from her children, whether they lived on the banks of the Nile or the Seine. I myself used to imagine, when I was in his salon, that I had suddenly been transported to Paris—the French furniture, the French people present, the French language spoken, and the French cuisine. Many French intellectuals did not know him except as a singular fancier of French art, or as a composer of passionate verse in the fine Gallic tongue. As for me, I knew him only this way—as a lover of France, a fanatic for her culture, and a preacher of her policies.

On that fateful day, I was sitting at the Pasha's side when M. Saroux said, while scrutinizing a two-inch bronze bust with his crossed and bulging eyes, "You fortunate man, your palace needs but a trifling change to turn it into complete museum."

"I certainly agree," the doctor ventured, tugging at his beard contemplatively, "for it is a permanent exhibit of all the schools of genius combined, with an obvious Francophile tendency."

The Pasha chimed in, "Its greatest virtue is in my balanced taste, which moves equally between the various trends, treating the rigid views of the differing schools all the same. And which strives for the enjoyment of beauty—whether its creator be Praxiteles or Raphael or Cézanne—with the exception of radical modern contrivances."

As I spoke, I glanced covertly at M. Saroux, teasing whom always delighted me, and said, "If the Ministry of Education could move this salon to the Higher College of Fine Arts, then they wouldn't waste money sending study missions to France and Italy."

M. Saroux laughed, swiveling to address me, "Then maybe they could save on the French headmaster, as well!"

But the Pasha said seriously, "Be assured, my dear Saroux, that if it were possible for this museum to leave Upper Egypt, then it would be heading straight for Paris."

We stared at him with surprise, as if we did not believe our ears. In truth, the Pasha's art collection was worth hundreds of thousands of Egyptian pounds—all of which had flowed into French pockets. It was stunning that he would think of donating it to France. While we were entitled to rejoice and be glad at this idea, nonetheless I could not restrain myself from asking:

"*Excellence,* is what you are saying true?"

The Pasha answered calmly, "Yes, my friend Dorian—and why not?"

M. Saroux broke in, "How deservedly happy and jubilant we

French should be! But I must tell your Excellency sincerely that I fear this may bring you a great many troubles."

When I seconded M. Saroux's view, the Pasha shifted his blue eyes back and forth between us with a sarcastic expression, and asked in feigned ignorance, "But why?"

Without hesitation, I said, "The press would find that quite a subject!"

"There is no doubt that the nationalist press is your old enemy," said Dr. Pierre. "Have you forgotten, Your Excellency, their biased attacks against you, and their accusations that you squander the money of the Egyptian peasants in France without any accountability?"

The Pasha sighed in dismissal, "The money of the peasants!"

Apologetically, the doctor hastened to add, "Please forgive me, Pasha—this is what they say."

Pursing his lips, His Excellency shrugged his shoulders disdainfully, as he adjusted his gold-rimmed spectacles over his eyes, saying, "I pay no heed to these vulgar voices of denunciation. And so long as my artistic conscience is ill at ease with leaving these miracles amidst this bestial people, then I will not permit them to be entombed here forever."

I knew my friend the Pasha's opinion of the Egyptians and his contempt for them. It is said in this regard that the year before, a gifted Egyptian physician, who had attained the title of "Bey," came to him, asking for the hand of his daughter. The Pasha threw him out brutally, calling him "the peasant son of a peasant." Despite my concordance with many of the Pasha's charges against his countrymen, I could not follow his thinking to its end.

"Your Excellency is a very harsh critic," I told him.

The Pasha giggled, "You, my dear Dorian, are a man who has given his entire, precious life to the past. Perhaps in its gloom you caught the flash of the genius that inspired the ancients, and it has inflamed your sympathy and affection for their descendants. You must not forget, my friend, that the Egyptians are the people who eat broad beans. "

Laughing too, I bantered back, "I'm sorry, Your Excellency, but do you not know that Sir Mackenzie, professor of English language at the Faculty of Arts, has recently declared that he has come to prefer broad beans to pudding?"

The Pasha laughed again, and so did we all with him. Then His Excellency said, "You know what I mean, but you like to jest. The Egyptians are genial animals, submissive in nature, of an obedient disposition. They have lived as slaves on the crumbs from their rulers' banquets for thousands of years. The likes of these have no right to be upset if I donate this museum to Paris."

"We are not speaking about what is right or not right, but about reality—and the reality is that they *would* be upset about it," said Saroux. "And their newspapers will be upset about it along with them," he added, in a meaningful tone.

Yet the Pasha displayed not the slightest concern. He was by nature scornful of the outcry of the masses, and the deceitful screams of the press. Perhaps due to his Turkish origins, he had the great defect of clinging to his own conceptions, his pertinacity, and his condescension toward Egyptians. He did not want to prolong the discussion, but closed the door upon it with his rare sense of subtlety. He kept us occupied for an hour sipping his delicious French coffee—there was none better in Egypt. Then the Pasha peered at me with interest, "Are you not aware, M. Dorian, that I have begun to compete with you in the discovery of hidden treasures?"

I looked at him quizzically and asked, "What are you saying, *Excellence?*"

The Pasha, laughing, pointed outdoors through the salon's window, "Just a short distance from us, in my palace garden, there is a magnificent excavation in progress."

Our interest was immediately obvious. I expected to hear a momentous announcement, for the word "excavation" prompts a special stimulus in me. I have spent an enormous part of my life—before I took up my post at the university—digging and sifting through the rich, magical earth of Egypt.

Still smiling, the Pasha continued, "I hope that you will not all make fun of me, my dear sirs, for I have done what the ancient kings used to do with sorcerers and masters of legerdemain. I don't know how I yielded to it, but there is no cause for regret, for a bit of superstition relieves the mind of the weight of facts and rigorous science. The gist of the story is this. Two days ago, a man well-known in this area, named Shaykh Jadallah—whom the people here respect and revere as a saint (and how many such saints do we have in Egypt!)—came to me, to insist on a peculiar request. And I acceded to it, amazing as it was.

"The man hailed me, in his own manner, and informed me that he had located—by means of his spiritual knowledge and through ancient books—a priceless treasure in the heart of my garden. He beseeched me to let him uncover it, under my supervision, tempting me with gold and pearls, if I would but gratify his wish. He was so annoying that I considered tossing him out. But he begged and pleaded with me until he wept, saying: 'Do not mock the science of God, and do not insult his favored believers!' I laughed a long time—until I had a sudden thought, and said to myself, 'Why don't I humor the man in his fantasy and go along with him in his belief? I wouldn't lose anything, and I would gain a certain type of amusement.' And so I did, my friends, and gave the man my permission.

34

"And now, in all seriousness I show him to you—he who he is digging in my garden, with two of my faithful servants assisting in his arduous labor. What do you think?"

The Pasha said all this with considerable mirth: we all laughed again with him. But as for myself, I recalled an incident similar to this one, "Naturally, you don't believe in the science of Shaykh Jadallah. Nor can I believe in it, either—more's the pity. But I also cannot forget that I discovered the tomb of the High Priest Kameni because of this same superstition!"

The amazement was plain on the faces of those present, and the Pasha queried me, "Professor, is what you are saying true?"

"Yes, Pasha, one day a shaykh like Shaykh Jadallah came to me in a place near the Valley of the Kings. He said that he had found, by means of his books and knowledge, the whereabouts of a treasure there. We kept pounding away in that spot, and—before the day was out—we found Kameni's tomb. This was, without a doubt, one of the most brilliant of coincidences."

Dr. Pierre laughed ironically, "Why do you credit that to coincidence, and deny the ancient science? Isn't it conceivable that the pharaohs bequeathed to their descendants their hidden secrets, just as they passed on to them their appearance and their customs?"

We kept on distracting ourselves with this sort of chatter, flitting from one topic to another, passing the time in great pleasure. And just before sunset, the guests took their leave. But I announced my wish to observe the excavation that Shaykh Jadallah was conducting in the garden. So we all left the salon, walking through the rear door to bid our goodbyes. We had gone but a few steps when we could hear the sounds of a great uproar—and a group of the servants cut across our path. We saw that they were holding a Sa'idi man, an Upper Egyptian, by his collar, giving him a sound beating with their fists. They dragged him roughly up to the Pasha, and one of them said, "Your Excellency, we caught this thief stealing Beamish's food."

I knew Beamish quite well—he was the Pasha's beloved dog, the most precious creature of God to his heart after his wife and children. He lived a spoiled and honored life in the Pasha's palace—attended by the staff and servants, and visited by a veterinarian once every month. Each day he was presented with meat, bones, milk, and broth—this wasn't the first time that the Sa'idis had pounced on Beamish's lunch.

The thief was an unmixed Upper Egyptian, marked by the looks of the ancients themselves. It was clear from his dress that he was wretchedly poor. The Pasha fixed him with a vicious stare, interrogating him gruffly, "Whatever induced you to violate the sanctity of my home?"

The man replied in fervent entreaty, panting from his efforts to fight off the servants, "I was starving, Your Excellency, when I saw the cooked meat scattered on the grass. My resistance failed me—I haven't tasted meat since the Feast of the Sacrifice!"

Turning to me, the Pasha exclaimed, "Do you see the difference between your unfortunates and ours? Your poor are propelled by hunger into stealing baguettes, while ours will settle for nothing less than cooked meat."

Then, raising his cane in the air, he wheeled back upon the thief and struck him hard on the shoulder, shouting to the servants, "Take him to the watchman!"

As the man was handed over, Dr. Pierre laughed, inquiring of the Pasha, "What will you do tomorrow if the natives get a whiff of the heaps of gold in the treasure of Shaykh Jadallah?"

The Pasha replied instantly, "I'll surround it with a wall of sentries, like the Maginot Line!"

We—the Pasha and I—bade the others farewell, and I followed him silently to where Shaykh Jadallah seemed about to transform himself into a great archaeologist. He was a man completely absorbed in his work—he and his helpers alike. They hacked at the earth with their hoes, lifting the dirt with baskets and throwing it aside. Shaykh Jadallah—his eyes flashing with a sharp gleam of hope and resolve, his scrawny arms charged with an unnatural strength—was nearing his goal, to which his divine insight had guided him. To me, his anomalous person represented Man in his activity, in his belief, and in his illusions—for the truth is that we create for ourselves gods and hallucinations, yet we believe in them in an extraordinary fashion. Our belief makes worlds for us of extreme beauty and creativity. Did not the ancestors of Shaykh Jadallah—whose face reminds me of the famous statue of an ancient Egyptian scribe—make humanity's first civilization? Did they not create loveliness equally on the surface of the earth, and beneath it? Were they not inspired in their work and their thought by Osiris and Amon? And what is Osiris, and what is Amon? Nothing much, on the whole. As for their civilization, it could be compared with—indeed, it *is*—our own civilization today.

We stood about watching the devout old shaykh. The Pasha smiled derisively, while I was sunk in my dreams. Neither us knew what Fate had concealed from us under those piles of dust. The labor appeared fruitless, and the Pasha grew bored. He suggested that we sit on the veranda—I followed him quietly. But we had hardly reached the stairs when Shaykh Jadallah ran up to intercept us, gasping from his gap-toothed mouth, "My lord . . . my lord . . . come and look!"

We turned toward him automatically. My heart was beating queerly from the Shaykh's appeal. He reminded me of his old counterpart who had cleaved my life between failure and success, between despair and hope. We hurried down the stairs, because the man had gone back the way he came—we both followed him, fighting our wish to run.

We found the three men moving a huge stone, approximately a square meter in size. As we drew nearer to them, we saw that the stone covered an opening of similar dimensions. I glanced at the Pasha, and he looked at me with eyes filled with astonishment and stupefaction. We then looked into the opening and saw a small staircase that ended in a corridor that led to the interior, parallel to the surface of the ground. The sun was about to go down, so I said to the Pasha, "Let's have a lantern." He sent a servant to fetch one. The man returned with the lantern, and I ordered him to walk before us. But he balked; I considered seizing the lamp from him. Shaykh Jadallah, however, reached him before me. He seized the man by the hand, reciting verses from the Qur'an and strange incantations. Then, surefootedly, the shaykh went down; I followed him, and the two restive servants followed behind.

We found ourselves in an underground passage no more than ten meters in length. Its ceiling hung several inches over our heads. The ground was simply soil, but the walls were granite. We advanced in slow steps until we met a stone door that blocked the path to intruders. Its appearance was not unfamiliar to me, nor were the symbols carved in its center. I ran my eyes over it, then glanced at the Pasha—whom I told in a shaking voice:

"Your Excellency, you have discovered an ancient tomb—for here lies General Hor, one of the most powerful figures in the Eighteenth Dynasty."

Violently piqued, Shaykh Jadallah declared, "Behind this door are riches—so says the book that does not lie!"

I shrugged my shoulders, "Call it what you will, the important thing is to open it."

"Opening the treasure is hard," the shaykh rejoined. "The only way to smash down the door and make it yield is by long recitation, which I will start doing now. That will take until dawn—are you ritually clean?"

His speech greatly affected the two servants, who looked at their master with embarrassment. They believed that they were soon to find themselves in the presence of the hidden power—but there was no time for ablution and the incantation of prayer. I reproved the shaykh firmly, "We didn't reach this door through recitation, so it seems more fitting to open it by force, as we did the one that came before it."

The shaykh was about to object, but could find no basis to do so, while the Pasha upbraided him. I kept quiet, as the shaykh looked at me askance. They resumed work once more: I snapped out of my reverie and set to work with them, until the insurmountable obstacle was sundered—and we found before us an opening into Hor's place of eternal rest.

As I was an expert at this sort of work, I directed them to stay in their places a while until the air had recirculated. For all of us together, it was a tense hour of waiting. The Pasha was silent and confused like one caught in a powerful dream, while the two servants looked on earnestly at the man in whom they placed their faith. The shaykh was warning me of what might befall us because of my contempt for his beliefs. As for myself, I was perhaps imagining what my eyes would behold. "Do you conceive what could happen if you acquire such a great antiquity, one that would become the highlight of the immortal museum in Paris?" I mused.

Then I went inside. Behind me entered al-Arna'uti Pasha, followed by Shaykh Jadallah; the servants deemed it wiser to remain in the outer corridor. But when the light of the lamp vanished, and the place plunged into darkness, they both leapt inside and cowered in a corner.

The burial chamber was just as its exterior indicated—I have seen its like numerous times in the past. The sarcophagus was in its customary place: on its surface was an image of its owner in gold. Next to it were three life-sized statues, one of them of a man—most probably Hor himself. Another was of a woman; from its position next to the man, this was undoubtedly his wife. In front of them both was a statue of a young boy.

Across from them were some sealed boxes, plus a number of colored vessels, chairs, tables, and military tackle. The walls were covered with paintings, signs, and inscriptions.

I shot a quick, awed glance over that now-resurrected world, but the Pasha did not leave me to my musings. He said to me—in what I did not know would be his last spoken words in this life, "The most appropriate thing, Professor Dorian, would be to inform the government about this matter immediately."

I sensed the defeat of my hopes, as I replied, "Wait a little, Pasha, while I make a quick appraisal."

With the Pasha to my right, I approached the boxes and furnishings, continuing to scrutinize them with expert, covetous eyes. My soul urged me to open them and to see their contents. I believed that they were filled with food, clothes, and jewelry, but it was very difficult for someone like me to control his will in the presence of those majestic artifacts that overwhelmed my heart with passion and emotion. And let us not forget the sarcophagus and the statues and the mummy—how bewitching was their allure!

I was awakened again from my fantasies when I heard the crude voice of Shaykh Jadallah shouting "Hush!" I turned toward him, hopping with rage—the least whisper at that time gravely affected my nerves. But then the shaykh blurted idiotically, "A sparrow!"

"What sparrow is this, O shaykh! Is this the time for jokes?" I rebuked him.

"I saw a sparrow fluttering its wings over the sarcophagus," he insisted.

We looked at the sarcophagus but saw nothing there. It would have been ludicrous to question the servants, so I told the obsolete holy man, "Spare us your delusions, Shaykh Jadallah."

Then I laughed, exclaiming to the Pasha in French, "Perhaps it was the *ka*—the soul of the deceased—come to pay him a visit with us."

I returned to perusing the boxes and the walls, which conversed with my heart in a silent language that only I could comprehend. Yet I could not give them my complete attention—for I soon heard the voices of the servants shrieking in terror, "Your Excellency—Pasha!"

We looked over at them quickly with wrath and exasperation— but only to find them in a bizarre state of horror, each grabbing onto the other. Their eyes widened and bulged wildly out of their heads, gazing stiff as the dead in the direction of the sarcophagus. Shaykh Jadallah was frozen where he stood, his hand trembling on the lamp, his eyes never moving from the same object. I looked at the sarcophagus and forgot my ire—for I saw its lid rising, and the mummy lying before us in its wrappings . . .

What is this? How was the sarcophagus opened? Have I been so influenced by my long residence in the Orient that my eye has been traduced—to this absurd degree—by its illusions and sleight of hand? But what sleight of hand is this? I see the mummy in front of me—and I am not the only one to see it. And how the Pasha has turned into a statue! And how these three men seem about to die with extreme fear and fright! What hallucination is this?

The truth is that I feel shame each time that circumstances compel me to tell what happened next—for I normally recount it to rational, well-educated people who have studied Taylor and Levy-Bruhl and Durkheim. But what can I do? Descartes himself,

41

if he were then in my place, would not have dared to dismiss his own senses.

What did I see?

I saw the mummy stir and sit up in his sarcophagus with a swift, nimble movement that would be impossible for a drunken man or one heavy from sleep, to say nothing of a corpse just roused from the world of the Dead. Then he bounded with a smoothly athletic motion—and stood erect facing us before the coffin.

My back was to the servants and Shaykh Jadallah, so I did not observe what was happening to them. But the light that illuminated the room was shaking with the hand that held it, while I fell into a state that beggars all description. I confess that my limbs rattled in a manner that I cannot convey—prey to a fear that I had never in my life experienced. Next to it, I cannot even recall the terror I felt in those harrowing days I spent on the Eastern Front and at the Battle of the Marne. How astonishing! Is that not a mummy there ahead? Or is that a corpse to which life has been restored by mysterious means? Or is that an Egyptian general who quivered with awe and submissiveness whenever he crossed the threshold of Pharaoh's palace?

Is it possible that such thoughts possessed me at that time? Nevertheless, I resisted this possession with all my might—for how can one be rightly guided by terror? I was mortally afraid. Yet my eyes were able to see even as my memory was able to preserve what my eyes saw.

I did not find before me a mere mummy, but a whole living man— complete in his manliness and vitality. His form reminded me of those images that one sees on so many temple walls. He was garbed in a white robe and a short loincloth, his great head covered with an elegant cowl. His broad chest was hung with many glittering honors. He was dignified, dreadful, of an imposing height. But, with all of his daunting splendor, it seemed to me that I had seen him before. I remembered the Sa'idi that the servants dragged to the Pasha and accused of stealing the dog Beamish's food. The resemblance was unnerving, but it was confined to his stature and color, not to his spirit and liveliness. Yet if this being right before me did not display such majesty and nobility, than perhaps I would be seized by doubts.

All the while, Hor fixed the Pasha in a cruel glare that he did not lift from him, as though he saw nothing but him.

What should I say, gentlemen? Yet I heard him speak—my God, Hor *spoke* after a silence of three thousand years. But he spoke in that ancient language that Death had enfolded for more than a millennium. I will forget everything in the world before I forget a single word of what his tongue uttered.

He said to my luckless friend, the Pasha, in a voice whose equal in augustness I had never heard before—for I have not yet had the honor of conversing with kings:

"*Do you not know me, slave? Why are you not falling on your knees before me?*"

From the Pasha, I heard not a sound, nor could I shift my rigid stare toward him. But I heard the Mighty One, possessor of the overpowering voice, speak once more:

"*I did not feel the troubling captivity of Death until my soul saw the astounding things that take place in this world, while I was bound with the shackles of Eternity, unable to move. Nor could I go to you, because my life had ended, as Osiris had decreed. But you came to me on your own two feet. I am bewildered at how you could seduce yourself into doing this foolish thing. Madness and vanity have overtaken you. Do you not praise the gods that Death had intervened between us? What did you come to do here, servant? You aren't satisfied with robbing my sons—so you have come to plunder my tomb, as well? Speak, you slave!*"

But the poor man could say nothing . . . for he understood nothing . . . he appeared struck by paralysis. Life had stolen back into the long-dead mummy—as it abandoned the living Pasha.

The mummy, meanwhile, resumed his reproach:

"What's the matter with you—why do you not speak? Am I not Hor? Are you not my servant, Shanaq? Do you not recollect that I came to you in your northern country, during one of my victorious raids? Do you pretend not to know me, slave? Your white skin, which is the mark of servitude, gives you away—no matter how much you may deny it. What are these ridiculous clothes that you have on? And what is this false pride that you hide yourself behind?"

Hor evidently believed that the Pasha deliberately refused to reply—so he shouted, his veins swelling, his face scowling with anger:

"What has befallen you? What has befallen the earth that the lowly are made lords and the lords are laid low? The sovereigns are reduced to slaves, and the slaves raised to sovereigns? How can you, slave, own such a palace, while my sons sweat there as your servants? Where are our inherited traditions? Where are the divine laws? Is this some sort of mockery?"

Hor's rage intensified. His eyes turned a furious red. Sparks flew out of them, as he railed with a voice like pealing thunder:

"How could you be so insolent with my son, you slave? Indeed, you humiliated him with a harshness that proves the slave-like nature that your soul exudes. You struck him with your stick because he was hungry, and forced his brothers to beat him, as well. Do Egypt's children go without food? Woe unto you, abject one . . . ."

Hor had not quite finished his rant when he advanced, roaring like a lion, upon the Pasha—intent to make him his prey. But the hapless Pasha did not wait for him—he had lost his power to endure. He fell motionless upon the ground, while Hor's menace spread a new terror throughout the chamber that shattered our last shred of composure. Shaykh Jadallah instantly prostrated himself on his face, the lamp

44

going down with him—extinguishing its light, sending the room back
into gloom. I recoiled in shock, as if expecting a deadly blow, without
knowing from what direction it would strike my head. I stared into
the darkness, shivering with panic and alarm. My strength deserted
me, while, to my good fortune, I lost all consciousness—and absent-
ed myself from the world . . . .

My dear sirs . . . There are times when I am beset by confusion, when
I am wracked with doubt. So I ask myself, was what I saw real, or a
deception? Perhaps, at times, I have a tendency to lie to myself. Yet
each time that I incline towards disbelief, I am confronted by facts over
which I have no control. What do you say, for example, to the testi-
mony of Shaykh Jadallah, a living person ready and able to repeat to you
what I have relayed? And what is your reply to the two pathetic servants, who were driven insane? And what of the tomb of Hor, and the
now-deserted palace? And, above all else, what of the death of
Mahmoud Pasha al-Arna'uti—which all the readers of the press
remember with the utmost sense of wonder?

The Return of Sinuhe

The incredible news spread through every part of Pharaoh's palace. Every tongue told it, all ears listened eagerly to it, and the stunned gossips repeated it—that a messenger from the land of the Amorites had descended upon Egypt. He bore a letter to Pharaoh from Prince Sinuhe, who had vanished without warning all of forty years before—and whose disappearance itself had wreaked havoc in people's minds. It was said that the prince had pleaded with the king to forgive what had passed, and to permit him to return to his native land. There he would retire in quiet isolation, awaiting the moment of his death in peace and security. No sooner had everyone recalled the hoary tale of the disappearance of Prince Sinuhe, then they would revive the forgotten events and remember their heroes—who were now old and senile, the ravages of age carved harshly upon them.

In that distant time, the queen was but a young princess living in the palace of Pharaoh Amenemhat I—a radiant rose blooming on a towering tree. Her lively body was clothed in the gown of youth and the shawl of beauty. Gentleness illuminated her spirit, her wit blazed, her intelligence gleamed. The two greatest princes of the realm were devoted to her: the then crown prince (and present king) Senwosret

I, and Prince Sinuhe. The two princes were the most perfect models of strength and youth, courage and wealth, affection and fidelity. Their hearts were filled with love and their souls with loyalty, until each of the two became upset with his companion—to the point of rage and ruthless action. When Pharaoh learned that their emotional bond to each other and their sense of mutual brotherhood were about to snap, he became very anxious. He summoned the princess and—after a long discussion—he commanded her to remain in her own wing of the palace, and not to leave it.

He also sent for the two princes and said to them, with firmness and candor, "You two are but miserable, accursed victims of your own blind self-abandon in the pursuit of rashness and folly—a laughing-stock among your fellow princes and a joke to the masses. The sages have said that a person does not merit the divine term 'human' until he is able to govern his lusts and his passions. Have you not behaved like dumb beasts and love-struck idiots? You should know that the princess is still confused between the two of you—and will remain confused until her heart is inspired to make a choice. But I call upon you both to renounce your rivalry in an ironbound agreement that you may not break. Furthermore, you will be satisfied with her decision, whatever it may be, and you will not bear anything toward your brother but fondness and loyalty—both inwardly and outwardly. Now, are you finished with this business?"

His tone did not leave room for hesitation. The two princes bowed their heads in silence, as Pharaoh bid them swear to their pact and shake hands. This they did—then left with the purest of intentions.

It happened during this time that unrest and rebellion broke out among the tribes of Libya. Pharaoh dispatched troops to chastise them, led by Prince Senwosret, the heir apparent, who chose Prince Sinuhe to command a brigade. The army clashed with the Libyans at several places, besetting them until they turned their backs and fled. The two princes displayed the kind of boldness and bravery befitting their characters. They were perhaps about to end their mission when the heir apparent suddenly announced the death of his father, King Amenemhat I. When this grievous news reached Prince Sinuhe, it seemed to have stirred his doubts as to what the new king might intend toward him. Suspicion swept over him and drove him to despair—so he melted away without warning, as though he had been swallowed by the sands of the desert.

Rumors abounded about Sinuhe's fate. Some said that he had fled to one of the far away villages. Others held that he had been assassinated in Libya. Still others said that he had killed himself out of desperation over life and love. The stories about him proliferated for quite a long time. But eventually, the tongues grew tired of them, consigning them to the tombs of oblivion under the rubble of time. Darkness enveloped them for forty years—until at last came that messenger from the land of the Amorites carrying Prince Sinuhe's letter—awakening the inattentive, and reminding the forgetful.

King Senwosret looked at the letter over and over again with disbelieving eyes. He consulted the queen, now in her sixty-fifth year, on the affair. They agreed to send messengers bearing precious gifts to Prince Sinuhe in Amora, inviting him to come to Egypt safely, and with honor.

Pharaoh's messengers traversed the northern deserts, carrying the royal gifts straight to the land of the Amorites. Then they returned, accompanied by a venerable old man of seventy-five years. Passing the pyramids, his limbs trembled, and his eyes were darkened by a cloud of distress. He was in bedouin attire—a coarse woolen robe with sandals. A sword scabbard girded his waist; a long white beard flowed down over his chest. Almost nothing remained to show that he was an Egyptian raised in the palace of Memphis, except that when the sailors' songs of the Nile reached his ears, his eyes became dreamy, his parched lips quivered, his breath beat violently in his breast—and he wept. The messengers knew nothing but that the old man threw himself down on the bank of the river and kissed it with ardor, as though he were kissing the cheek of a sweetheart from whom he had long been parted.

They brought him to Pharaoh's palace. He came into the presence of King Senwosret I, who was seated before him, and said, "May the Lord bless you, O exalted king, for forgiving me—and for graciously allowing me to return to the sacred soil of Egypt."

Pharaoh looked at him closely with obvious amazement, and said, his voice rising, "Is that really you? Are you my brother and the companion of my childhood and youth—Prince Sinuhe?"

"Before you, my lord, is what the desert and forty years have done to Prince Sinuhe."

Shaking his head, the king drew his brother toward him with tenderness and respect, and asked, "What did the Lord do with you during all these forty years?"

The prince pulled himself up straight in his seat, and began to tell his tale.

"My lord, the story of my flight began at the hour that you were informed of our mighty father's death out in the Western Desert. There the Devil blinded me and evil whispers terrified me. So I threw myself into the wind, which blew me across deserts, villages, and rivers, until I passed the borders between damnation and madness. But in the land of exile, the name of the person whose face I had fled, and who had dazzled me with his fame, conferred honor upon me. And whenever I confronted trouble, I cast my thoughts back to Pharaoh—and my cares left me. Yet I remained lost in my wanderings, until the leader of the Tonu tribes in Amora learned of my plight, and invited me to see him.

"He was a magnificent chief who held Egypt and its subjects in all awe and affection. He spoke to me as a man of power, asking me about my homeland. I told him what I knew, while keeping the truth about myself from him. He offered me marriage to one of his daughters, and I accepted—and began to despair that I would ever again see my homeland. After a short time, I—who was raised on Pharaoh's famous chariots, and grew up in the wars of Libya and Nubia—was able to conquer all of Tonu's enemies. From them I took prisoners, their women and goods, their weapons and spoils, and their herds, and my status rose even further. The chief appointed me the head of his armies, making me his expected successor.

"The gravest challenge that I faced was the great thief of the desert, a demonic giant—the very mention of whom frightened the bravest of men. He came to my place seeking to seize my home, my wife, and my wealth. The men, women, and children all rushed to the square to see this most ferocious example of combat between two opponents. I stood against him amidst the cheers and apprehension, fighting him for a long time. Dodging a mighty blow from his axe, I launched my piercing arrow and it struck him in the neck. Fatally weakened, he fell to the ground, death rattling in his throat. From that day onward, I was the undisputed lord of the badlands.

"Then I succeeded my father-in-law after his death, ruling the tribes by the sword, enforcing the traditions of the desert. And the days, seasons, and years passed by, one after another. My sons grew into strong men who knew nothing but the wilderness as the place for birth, life, glory, and death. Do you not see, my lord, that I suffered in my estrangement from Egypt? That I was tossed back and forth by horrors and anxieties, and was afflicted by calamities, although I also enjoyed love and the siring of children, reaping glory and happiness along the way. But old age and weakness finally caught up with me, and I conceded authority to my sons. Then I went home to my tent to await my passing.

"In my isolation, heartaches assailed me, and anguish overwhelmed me, as I remembered gorgeous Egypt—the fertile playground of my childhood and youth. Desire disturbed me, and longing beckoned my heart. There appeared before my eyes scenes of the Nile and the luxuriant greenery and the heavenly blue sky and the mighty pyramids and the lofty obelisks, and I feared that death would overtake me while I was in a land other than Egypt.

"So I sent a messenger to you, my lord, and my lord chose to pardon me and to receive me hospitably. I do not wish for more than a quiet corner to live out my old age, until Sinuhe's appointed hour comes round. Then he would be thrown into the embalming tank, and in his sarcophagus, the Book of the Dead—guide to the afterlife—would be laid. The professional women mourners of Egypt would wail over him with their plaintive rhyming cries . . . ."

Pharaoh listened to Sinuhe with excitement and delight. Patting his shoulder gently, he said, "Whatever you want is yours." Then the king summoned one of his chamberlains, who led the prince into his wing of the palace.

Just before evening, a messenger came, saying that it would please the queen if she could meet with him. Immediately, Sinuhe rose to go to her, his aged heart beating hard. Following the messenger, nervous and distracted, he muttered to himself, "O Lord! Is it possible that I will see her once again? Will she really remember me? Will she remember Sinuhe, the young prince and lover?"

He crossed the threshold of her room like a man walking in his sleep. He reached her throne in seconds. Lifting his eyes up to her, he saw the face of his companion, whose youthful bloom the years had withered. Of her former loveliness, only faint traces remained.

Bowing to her in reverence, he kissed the hem of her robe. The queen then spoke to him, without concealing her astonishment, "My God, is this truly our Prince Sinuhe?"

The prince smiled without uttering a word. He had not yet recovered himself, when the queen said, "My lord has told me of your conversation. I was impressed by your feats, and the harshness of your struggle, though it took me aback that you had the fortitude to leave your wife and children behind."

"Mercy upon you, my queen," Sinuhe replied. "What remains of my life merely lengthens my torture, while the likes of me would find it unbearable to be buried outside of dear Egypt."

The woman lowered her gaze for a moment, then raising up to him her eyes filled with dreams, she said to him tenderly, "Prince Sinuhe, you have told us your story, but do you know ours? You fled at the time that you learned of Pharaoh's death. You suspected that your rival, who had the upper hand, would not spare your life. You took off with the wind and traversed the deserts of Amora. Did you not know how your flight would injure yourself and those that you love?"

Confusion showed on Sinuhe's face, but he did not break his silence. The queen continued, "Yet how could you know that the heir apparent visited me just before your departure at the head of the campaign in Libya. He said to me: 'Princess, my heart tells me that you have chosen the man that you want. Please answer me truthfully, and I promise you just as truthfully that I will be both contented and loyal. I would never break this vow.'"

Her majesty grew quiet. Sinuhe queried her with a sigh, "Were you frank with him, my queen?"

She answered by nodding her head, then her breath grew more agitated. Sinuhe, gasping from the forty-year voyage back to his early manhood, pressed her further.

"And what did you tell him?"

"Will it really interest you to know my answer? After a lapse of forty years? And after your children have grown to be chiefs of the tribes of Tonu?"

His exhausted eyes flashed a look of perplexity, then he said with a tremulous voice, "By the Sacred Lord, it matters to me."

She was staring at his face with pleasure and concern, and said, smiling, "How strange this is, O Sinuhe! But you shall have what you want. I will not hold back the answer that you should have heard forty years ago. Senwosret questioned me closely, so I told him that I would grant him whatever I had of fondness and friendship. But as for my heart . . . ."

The queen halted for a moment, as Sinuhe again looked up, his beard twitching, shock and dismay bursting on his face. Then she resumed, "As for my heart—I am helpless to control it. "

"My Lord," he muttered.

"Yes, that is what I said to Senwosret. He bid me a moving good-bye—and swore that he would remain your brother so long as he breathed.

"But you were hasty, Sinuhe, and ran off with the wind. You strangled our high hopes, and buried our happiness alive. When the news of your vanishing came to me, I could hardly believe it—I nearly died of grief. Afterwards, I lived in seclusion for many long years. Then, at last, life mocked at my sorrows; the love of it freed me from the malaise of pain and despair. I was content with the king as my husband. This is my story, O Sinuhe."

She gazed into his face to see him drop his eyes in mourning; his fingers shook with emotion. She continued to regard him with compassion and joy, and asked herself: "Could it be that the agony of our long-ago love still toys with this ancient heart, so close to its demise?"

A Voice from the Other World

1

By God, what does this tomb want for the good things of a bygone existence? It is a fragment of life's essence rich with lusciousness and luxury. Its walls are adorned with scenes of servants and slave girls. It is filled with the most lavish of furniture, the most sublime of embellishments. It has all that one could want of splendid fixtures and fragrances and decorative objects. It has a storehouse stuffed with seeds, fruits, and vegetables, and what my library bore of books filled with wisdom, and what a writer may need from the tools of his trade. It is the world as I knew it. But do my senses now still taste life? Do I still need its distractions? Those who built this house for the dead surely labored in vain. And yet, I cannot deny, however strange it may seem, that I have not lost the urge to write. How amazing! What are these leaves that call to me with their beloved bewitchment? Is there still some part of me from which Death has not obliterated the desires of weakness and passion? Have we, the community of scribblers, been sentenced to suffer for our deeds in both of our lives? In any case, a period of waiting still lies before me, after which I shall begin my journey into eternity. So let me occupy this idle time with the reed pen, for how often has this instrument enhanced my precious hours of leisure.

O Lord! Do I not still remember the day that rent my world between life and death? Yes, on that day I left the Prince's palace just before sunset, after exhausting efforts which had utterly absorbed me, until the Prince said to me, "Taw-ty, that's enough work—don't wear yourself out." The sun was slanting toward the western horizon, the endless expanse of the realm of shadows. The flickerings of its fading rays shook with the shiver of Death upon the surface of the sacred Nile. I continued on my accustomed way, across from the sycomore tree at the southern edge of the village where my lovely house lies.

O holy Amon! What is this aching in my joints and my bones? It's not a result of my efforts at work, for how often have I worked without a pause, and how often have I zealously persevered and patiently carried on and prevailed over fatigue by force and resolve! What is this consuming pain? And what is this powerful trembling—a new and unexpected thing? I am filled with fear. Could this be the malaise that does not descend upon the body until the condition is fatal? Fold up, village road—for I lack the strength to draw any charm from your beauty!

Be gone, you omen of heaven, for in Taw-ty's breast there is no wish to summon you! I kept going down the road in dread of where it would end. At my home's doorstep the face of my wife—the companion of my youth and the mother of my children—loomed before me. "My poor Taw-ty, why are you quivering so? Why do your eyes look so distressed?" she cried. I said to her, in agony and despair, "O sister! Something unthinkable has occurred. A deadly disease has settled in the body of your husband. Make ready the bed and cover me up. Summon the physician and our children and loved ones, and tell them that Taw-ty is on his bed, pleading to his Lord, and to plead along with him for his cure."

She who had taken me to her breast carried me, and the doctor came to give me medicine. Pointing to heaven, he said, "O great writer Taw-ty, O servant of His Majesty the Prince, you are in need of the Lord's compassion. Pray to Him from the depths of your heart!" And I lay there, without strength or resource. O Divine Amon, whose wisdom is lofty! Did I not accompany His Highness the Prince to the north in the armies of Pharaoh? Did I not witness the fighting in the deserts of Zahi and Nubia? Was I not there at Qadesh in the courageous campaign? Indeed, O Lord, and I was delivered from the lances and the chariots and the battles. So how can Death threaten me in my dear, safe village, in the embrace of my spouse and my mother and my children? Meanwhile I drowned in the vapors of fever, as my dizziness increased. Senseless jabber flowed from my tongue, and I felt the hand of Doom moving for my heart. How cruel you are, O Death! I see you advancing toward your target on two sure feet, with a heart made of stone. You do not tire or weary, tears do not sway you, you do not show mercy, nor do hopes arouse your sympathy. You trample our tiny hearts, you disregard our desires and dreams—and you do not change your appointed ways even when your prey is in the blooming spring of youth. Taw-ty is in his twenty-sixth year, the father of sons and daughters—do you not hear? What would it harm you if you left my breath to recurr in my breast? Send for me when I have been sated with this beautiful and beloved life. It has not brought me torment, nor have I abstained from it ever. I have loved it from the depth of my heart—and it is still in its prime. My health has been good, my money plentiful, my aspirations unbounded. Haven't you noted all these things? Around me are hearts full of affection, souls and deities—haven't you looked into their tearful eyes? It's as if I haven't lived one hour of this alluring life. What did I see of its scenes? What have I heard of its voices? And what have I learned of its sciences? What have I tasted of its arts? Which of its colors shall fade? What opportunities shall be lost tomorrow? What raptures shall be extinguished? What passions shall abate? What delights shall disappear?

I recalled this, all of it. In my eternity, other things, without boundaries or limits, that lay between the enchantments of the past, the magic of the present and the longings of the future, spun before me. The flowers and fields and waters and clouds and food and drink and songs and ideas and love and my children and the Prince's palace and Pharaoh's parties and the money I was paid and the medals and titles and the honors and the glory, were drawn before my senses. And I wondered, would all this vanish into the void?

My breast pounded heavily; I was filled with sadness and grief, and every afflicted part of me shouted, "I do not want to die!" The legions of night followed in succession, and sleep overcame the little ones. My wife lingered about my head, my mother about my feet. Midnight came and as quickly passed while we remained in this state, until the baying of jackals startled me with the blue light of dawn. A bizarre feeling of alarm seized me, as a sinister silence settled over all. Then I felt my mother's hand gripping my feet as she called in a quavering voice, "My son, my son!" My wife screamed, "Taw-ty, what do you see?" But I was unable to reply. Something, no doubt, aroused their apprehension. Did she see what this was? Did the warning show on my face? My gaze shifted against my will to the entrance of the room. The door was locked, yet the Messenger entered. He entered without needing to open the door. I knew him without knowing him before: he was the Messenger of the Hereafter, without any like him. He approached me in awesome silence and irresistible beauty. As he did so my eyes were fixed upon him; he was all I could see. I wanted to call out to him but my tongue would not obey. He seemed to know my inner desire, for his smile grew broader, and I recognized him as my escort, while nothing else remained in my mind.

The whisperings of night and my agonies and infirmities all passed away, and I ignored the tears all around me, as I found myself in a state of well-being and security that I had never before experienced. I yielded myself to an infinite love, leaving my body alone in the struggle! I saw, without any anxiety, the blood in my veins resisting, my heart beating and straining, my muscles tightening and slackening, my breath deeply panting, my chest rising and falling. I felt the hands of affection lift my back and enfold me, and I saw my insides and my outside without any care or concern. Then the Messenger seemed to turn his attention from me to my body directly, to execute his mission with confidence and assurance, and a smile that did not leave his two handsome lips. And I saw the holy aura of life surrender to his will, and depart from my feet and my calves and my thighs and my belly and my chest, and the blood within them freeze and the limbs stiffen and the heart stop, until a deep sigh escaped my gaping mouth. My corpse became quiet as I sank into eternity, and the Messenger took his leave just as he came to me, without anyone's noticing. A peculiar feeling pervaded me that I had left life behind, that I had ceased to dwell among the people of the world

2

The stunning sensation that I had actually died, that I no longer belonged to the realm of the living, truly overwhelmed me. I was still in my room, and the room was still as it was, so what had happened? What had changed within me? My mother and my wife were leaning over my body, when something occurred that I could not doubt, and it was the most critical thing of all. I was not surprised, and if I had been able to reply to my wife when she asked me, "Taw-ty, what do you see?" I would have said, "I am dying." But I had lost the power of speech and of other things. I was not surprised, as I have said, when I felt the depths of Death—as the bed feels the numbing flow of sleep—completely aware of what was happening. What could not be doubted is that Death is neither painful nor terrifying, as mortals imagine. If they knew the truth about it, they would seek it out as they do well-aged wine, preferring it over all others. For it is not regret or sadness that grips the dying person. Rather, life appears as something paltry and unimportant when one intuits on the horizon that divine and joyous light. I was shackled with fetters, then they were smashed. I was trapped inside a vessel, then I was set free. I was intensely heavy on the earth, then I shed my bonds and was rid of my weight. My form was narrow, then I stretched everywhere outward without any bounds. My senses were limited, then each faculty changed utterly; I could see all and I could hear all and I could comprehend all, and I could perceive all at once what was above me and below me and around me—as if I had left my body sprawled before me to take from Creation an entirely new one. This total transformation that defies description took place in an instant. Yet, I still felt that I had not quit the room that had witnessed the happiest moments of my previous existence. It was as though I had been made custodian of my former body until it reached its final rest.

So I continued to observe everything around me calmly and attentively, without apprehension. The air of the room was enveloped in pain and dejection, while my mother and wife persisted in working together over my body—my old companion—with its familiar features, lying motionless on the bed. Meanwhile, its color had gone white tinged with blue, its eyelids closed, and its limbs went limp. The children and the servants kept calling to it; they all wept and cried. Those in attendance poured copious tears over it, until heartache, sorrow, and gloom seemed to consume them. All the time I watched them with an odd indifference, as if never for a day had I been close to them. What is this dead body? Why are these humans howling about it so? What is this misfortune that has made their faces ugly and distorted? No, I am no longer one of the people of the world, and their tears and lamentations cannot restore me to it. I wished that all my ties with it would be cut so that I could hover about in my new domain, but, regrettably, my dear ones still held a part of my liberty captive to the temporal world, so I steeled myself with patience as I took up this burden. Then my mother came with a sheet to cover my cadaver, while the children and servants went out. She took my wife by the hand as they both left the room and locked the door behind them. Yet they remained in my sight, because the walls did nothing to impede my view. I saw them both as they removed their clothing and dressed in black for mourning. Next they headed toward the house's courtyard, loosening their braids and strewing dust over their heads, throwing off their sandals as they hurried toward the door. They rushed out shouting and beating the sides of their faces, while my mother kept callling "My son!" and my wife called out, "O my husband!" Then they both cried out together, "Mercy upon you, O poor Taw-ty—Death has taken you without compassion for your youth!"

They left the house in this condition of moaning and weeping, continuing along until they passed the first home on the way. There the mistress of the house came out to them in fright. "O Sisters, what is upsetting you?" she asked. The two women answered, "Our house is ruined! Our children are orphaned! The mother is bereaved! The wife is widowed! Mercy upon you, O Taw-ty!" So the woman bawled out from deep in her breast, "O heart dismayed! O youth deprived! O hopes destroyed!" And she followed the two women, all the while scattering dust on her own head and striking her cheeks. Each time they passed a house its mistress came out to join them, until all the women had flocked to their throng. A woman experienced in mourning led them onward, continually reciting my name and my virtues. On they went, cutting across all the streets in the village, bringing grief and desolation to every location. But this name of mine that the mourners were chanting, why did it not affect me at all?

Yes, this name had become as strange to me as my laid-out body. I kept wondering when, oh when, would all this end? Then, in the evening, the men came. As the wailing went up around us, they carried my body into the House of Embalming, and placed it on the slab in the Sacred Chamber. The room was long and very wide, without a single window save for a skylight in the center of the ceiling. The slab was in the center of the room, and on either side of it were shelves stocked with jars full of chemicals. In the middle, under the skylight, was a huge trough flowing with the miraculous fluid. The men went out, leaving only two behind. These two were experts, as testified by the speed and dexterity with which they worked. One of them came with a basin, which he set down close to the slab. They collaborated in stripping the cadaver of its clothing until every part of it was completely exposed. They did this quietly and without concern. Then the one who had brought the basin said, while feeling the muscles of my chest and arms, "He was a tough man, look!" And the other said, "He was Taw-ty, one of the Prince's men. In exchange for food and drink, he bravely undertook the hazards of war." The one who had brought the basin muttered cautiously, "What if one could borrow these bodies?" The other replied, laughing, "You old geezer, what good is a corpse?" But the man just said, while shaking his head, "He was a strong man, he truly was . . . ."

And so the other man, still laughing, took a long, sharp knife from one of the shelves, and said, "Let's see just how strong he is now!" He stabbed the left side of the breast with the blade, slicing his way down to the hip. Then he worked the insides with his hand, grabbing and pulling until he brought out the bowels and the stomach, and dropped them into the basin. Then he added the heart and the liver. In just a few moments, my entire internal organs were laid before me, as these men were embalmers of consummate skill. I inspected each organ with care, especially my stomach, which I knew to be strong and ever-active. Thanks to my magical powers of sight, I could view its contents clearly—the rice and figs and remains of the wine from the Prince's banquet last night. I recalled his remark when he beckoned me to the table, "Eat and drink, Tawty—may you enjoy life, most trustworthy man!" I saw and I remembered, without any feeling or effect, without any impact on my amazing indifference. Then I looked at my heart and saw a world filled with wonders: the ruins of passionate love, of sorrow and rage, the images of lovers and friends. And of enemies, for I had left my romantic ardor and the glory of its depths to display my courage in the wars of Zahi and Nubia. In these lands I had beheld horrifying scenes of carnage on the battlefield, of bloody, hacked-off limbs—the traces of a struggle unencumbered by mercy—until I added to my dynasty's land a plot which our neighbor had also coveted for a number of years. I saw in my heart the bulk of my life and the longings that had grieved me.

Meanwhile the man kept on working with coolness and precision.

He produced a pointed hook, which he shoved up my nose with great concentration, until he reached his objective. Then rapidly, with familiarity and violence, he forced out my big brain, which oozed away in a slimy stream, sending particles out into the air of what once had been my dazzling ideas, my dearest hopes, and the smoke of my dreams. These were my own thoughts that were painted before my eyes, but when I considered them in the light of the truth that my spirit now saw, they seemed no more than grotesque trivialities. The state in which I now found refuge tried hard to keep them out. How my head reeled from the effort!

Here I am, declaiming the poem that I had composed depicting the battle of Qadesh. And here are the speeches that I made before the Prince at public occasions, and here are my views on literature and good conduct, and the rules of astronomy that I memorized from the books of Qaqimna. All of these the man removed with the bits of my brain. They settled between the stomach and the intestines in the tub full of blood—not counting those parts which fell upon the ground to be squashed underfoot. "Now the body has been well cleaned!" the expert handling the hook pronounced. "When you die, may you find a hand as practiced as your own!" his friend added, giggling. At this the two technicians carried what remained of my body to the great trough filled with the magic liquid, immersing it within. Then they washed their hands and left the chamber. Meanwhile, I understood that the room would not be opened again for a span of seventy days—the period of embalming. I was touched with unease. The thought struck me that my spirit should go out into the world to catch a glimpse of my final farewell.

3

My soul was eager to go out into the world, and so I did. This did not entail actual movement as such, for it was enough that I simply direct my thoughts toward something and I would find it right in front of me. Yet the reality was even greater, for my sight became something truly extraordinary—nothing was beyond it. It turned into a penetrating power that passed through barriers and cut through veils, seeing into minds and hidden recesses. However, though our parting had been decreed, my thoughts were pulled toward my family, so I found myself back in my home. The children had gone into a deep sleep which the turbulence did not disturb. My mother and wife lay down on the floor, the misery and suffering plain on their faces from the force of their crying and sorrow. Tomorrow their woes would multiply even more when the sarcophagus would proceed to its perpetual place of burial. My spirit entered them and moved their heads and appeared before them in dreams, and I saw the two tortured hearts beating in agony and pain. What was all this worry? Something, however, attracted my vision. I saw in the dark oppression of each of their hearts a spot of white, and I knew it—for nothing was unknown to me—as the germ of forgetfulness. Oh! This germ would grow larger and spread wider until it covered the heart entire. Indeed, I saw all of this clearly, without being bothered, for nothing could trouble me now. Instead I wondered, intrigued by the taste of discovery, when might this happen? My two supernatural eyes brought me a picture from the future: I saw my mother take a young boy by her right hand and make her way through thickly crowded streets, waving a lotus flower. And I learned that she had come out—or that she would come out—to take part in our village's happiest festival, the feast of the goddess Isis. Her face was jubilant, and my son was hooting with laughter. I saw my wife prepare a banquet with food of the best kinds found in her world and invite a man that I knew to it. This was her maternal cousin Sa-wu—and what an excellent husband he was! If the dead could feel pleasure, then I would have been pleased for her. Sa-wu was a man of virtue, for he who makes happy my wife and tends well to my children is a good man indeed.

With this my spirit left my house, and I stopped on the wayside at the sweet Prince's palace. I peered into the Prince's consciousness and found him, who had appreciated me and prized me in the most moving manner, feeling sorry for my loss. His mind was preoccupied with choosing my successor. I read within his memory the name of the new candidate: Ab-Ra, one of my more promising subordinates, though we had not been intimate.

All this was fine. But why remain in my village today, when Pharaoh is to receive the envoy of the Hittites, come to sign a pact of peace and reconciliation? I saw Memphis, in a glance of the eye, clamoring with her teeming multitudes, and the palace at the height of its splendor. The King, the ambassador, the priests, the nobles, and the generals were gathered in the hall of the Great Throne. All of these masters of the world were met in one place. The triumphant monarch was speaking to the representative of the mighty Hittites with an air of warm civility. But the King's breast was filled with scorn, and a single expression recurred in his mind, "There's no avoiding the unavoidable." As for the envoy, his heart was brimming over with hate, and this thought was dammed up with it: "Be patient until this powerful ruler dies."

My eyes wandered everywhere. I saw the faces and the clothes and the hearts and the minds and the bellies. I saw the outer world and the inner one without any hindrance, and amused myself for a time by examining the exquisite food and the vintage wine in their stomachs until I came across onion and garlic in the gut of a priest. These are both forbidden for the clergy! I asked myself, do you see how this pious man takes advantage of his fellows' distraction to sneak down this food? In part of a nobleman's stomach, I caught the creep of the disease that would sap away his life. At this moment, the man was talking to a general with glee and delight. Inwardly, I said to him, "May you be welcome!" Then my sight fell on the governor Tety, infamous for his cruelty and ruthlessness, to the point that Pharaoh had to admonish him to be moderate in overseeing his province. I scrutinized him carefully, immediately discovering that his body was frail, his limbs were sick, and that he complained bitterly and ceaselessly about his teeth and his joints. Each time the pain assailed him, he yearned to be able to sever the infection from his body. This explained why he was gripped by cruelty, as he did not hesitate to cut out the crooked from among his subjects with merciless brutality. In addition to Tety, I saw the vizier, Mina. That obdurate man, who fought the idea of peace with all this force, was always agitating for war. Do you see the secret of this dangerous minister's stubbornness? I saw that his mind was brilliant but his bowels were feeble. The morsels of his food remained trapped in them a long time, corrupting his blood as it circulated, so that it reached his brain spoiled, fouling his reason. As a result, that which issued from his mouth possessed great evil! The man satisfied with his own opinion sees it as straight and rightly guided, though I saw his mind as blackened and polluted.

Next my vision turned to the breasts of those present, looking into their hidden corners and behind their grinning faces. One was horribly bored, whispering to his companion, "When can we go back to the palace to hear the courtesans sing?" And that one over there muttered, "If the man had died from his illness, I would now be commander of the spear-throwers brigade!" And this other one pondered to himself in anguish, "When will the imbecile leave for his tour of inspection, so that I may rush to be with his gorgeous wife, whom I adore—ahhh!" And yet another told a friend from his deepest heart, "A human being doesn't know when his appointed time will come." And, "After today, I will not put off building my tomb." Or, "Of what good is money, then?" Confusion so controlled his heart that he told a comrade, "Akhenaten said that the Lord is Aton, while Horemheb said that He was Amon. There is also a sect that worships Ra—so why did the Lord leave us in dissension?" I did not tarry too long at Pharaoh's magnificent party, for I soon succumbed to ennui. I turned away from it, to find myself once more abroad in the wide world.

Many scenes from the earth and the heavens passed before me. I grasped their essential truths, seeing into their deepest aspects, until I fixed upon an egg being fertilized in a womb. I beheld its flesh and bones forming, and watched its birth, while my vision ran with it towards its future. I saw it as a child, as a boy, as a youth, as a grown man, as an old man—and as a dead man. I saw the events that befell him, his pleasure and torment and contentment and anger and hope and despair and his health and his illness, his passion and his boredom. I saw all these together in just a minute, until the cries of his birth and the moans of his death were mingled together in my ears! A capricious desire to play overcame me, and I followed the lifetimes of many individuals from their birth to their demise. I savored enormously the flow of their different states of being, which were hardly divided in time. For here a face would laugh and then it would scowl and then guffaw and then frown tens and tens of times in a fraction of a second! This woman wanders about as a young beauty, then she falls in love and marries and becomes pregnant and has children and goes into senility and whithers away and becomes loathesome to look upon, all in a brief interval. Loyalty and treachery are not cleaved by an instant. These and countless other things are what make a farce of life—if the deceased could laugh, then I would drown in laughter. It seemed to me as though there is no reality in the world except for change. My soul wished that all these people and their crazy lives would just go away and be gone from my sight. I regarded them from afar as a numberless, limitless horde. Their forms diminished and their features dissolved and the distinctions between them disappeared. They became a single block, silent and still, without life or movement. I continued to stare at them in shock and perplexity, that slowly lessened by degrees until a new dimension was revealed to me that had previously been concealed.

I saw this calm darkness ignite with an all-encompassing light, as the faint, fading beams that pulsated in each brain, which by themselves were weak and dying, all clung to each other in one cohesive mass, emanating a powerful, dazzling incandescence. I saw in its radiance a gleaming truth, a pure goodness, and a luminous beauty, and my wonder and bewilderment returned. O Lord, no matter how the soul suffers and is tortured, it goes on inventing and creating just the same. And Lord, Taw-ty has seen glorious things and will see yet more glorious and awesome things. I became convinced that this light that glowed upon me was but a mere speck of the heaven to which I would ascend. I looked away and turned my back to the world, to find myself once again in the Sacred Chamber for embalming—and a divine ecstasy embued my spirit that cannot be conveyed.

The seventy days of embalming were done. The men came again. They removed my body from the trough and wrapped it in layers of cloth. They brought with them a sarcophagus, upon which an image of the youthful Taw-ty was most flatteringly engraved, and placed the body inside it. Then they hoisted it upon the back of their necks and filed outside, where they met my family and my neighbors, who struck their faces and wailed. Their shrieks were worse than those on the day my death was announced. They proceeded to the Nile and embarked on a huge boat, which bore them to the City of Immortality on the West Bank. They jostled about the sarcophagus, calling out and howling, "My tears will not dry, my heart knows no peace after you, Taw-ty!" while my wife entreated aloud, "O my husband, why was I condemned to live after you?"

The Prince's chamberlain declared, "O glorious writer, Taw-ty, you have left your place empty!"

For a long while I watched with these eyes that had forgotten their past, as if there were no ties that bound me to this world, nor with these humans. The boat pulled up to the shore, and they hoisted up the sarcophagus once more. From there they marched with it to the mausoleum—on which I had spent the best part of my treasure—and set it down in its intended place. During all this, a band of priests intoned some verses from the Book of the Dead, lecturing me on how to behave in the afterlife! Then they began to withdraw, one after another, until the tomb was deserted. There was nothing left to hear but the sound of distant mourning. The doors were sealed and sand shoveled over them. Thus perished all relations between the world that I had bid goodbye, and the world that I now greet . . . .

Note: Here the hieroglyphic text breaks off. Perhaps the period of waiting to which the writer referred at the start of this document had ended, or perhaps his voyage into Eternity had begun. There he would be diverted from his much-loved pen—and from all things.

Glossary

al-Arna'uti: In Arabic, 'the Albanian'—an allusion to the origins of the then-regnant Muhammad 'Ali dynasty, installed nominally under the Ottomans as rulers of Egypt in 1805. Much of the Egyptian aristocracy was subsequently of mixed Turkish–Albanian blood. The pasha in "The Mummy Awakens" is most likely based upon Mohamed Mahmoud Bey Khalil (1877–1953), a millionaire Francophile collector of art who was accused in the Egyptian press in the late 1930s of wanting to will his exquisite private gallery of mainly French paintings to the Louvre. It is now housed in his former mansion in Giza in a museum bearing his name.

Aswan: A city at the Nile's first cataract in Upper (southern) Egypt. Mahfouz here uses the pharaonic Egyptian name Abu (actually Elephantine Island at Aswan), which was the country's southern-most outpost on the border with ancient Nubia. The historical Userkaf's capital was at Mennufer (Memphis) close to present-day Cairo, rather than Aswan, though the royal annals of the Old Kingdom recorded on the Palermo Stone show that he kept a *per* (house, estate) at Abu. His only known pyramid—quarried into rubble in antiquity—was built near there, in northern Saqqara, rather than at Aswan.

Broad beans: Also called horse beans (and known as *ful* in Arabic), these are an indespensable part of the Egyptian diet.

Fuad I University: Named for King Ahmad Fuad I (r. 1917–36), who, as a prince, was one of its founders in 1908. The institution was renamed Cairo University after the Free Officers coup of 1952. Naguib Mahfouz earned a bachelor's degree in philosophy there in 1934 (when it was then called the Egyptian National University), where he briefly did postgraduate work, and served in the school's administration until 1939. During this time, he occasionally attended lectures in Egyptology, some of which were likely given by Prof. Etienne Marie-Felix Drioton (1889–1961), then head of Egypt's Department of Antiquities—and a probable model for Prof. Dorian in the story, "The Mummy Awakens."

'Id al-adha: The 'Feast of Sacrifice,' which commemorates Abraham's sacrifice of a ram in place of his son Isma'il, as related in the Qur'an. Muslims celebrate this several-day event (also known as Greater Bairam) by slaughtering animals on the first dawn of the feast, often distributing the meat to the poor.

Ka: In the complex system of pharaonic-era beliefs, when someone died, their *ka*, or spiritual essence, would come to visit the deceased. The *ka* brought with it the *ba*, the dead person's soul, depicted as a human-headed bird in mortuary reliefs, often sculpted sitting on the mummy. Strictly speaking, it was Hor's *ba*, not his *ka*, that was represented by the sparrow. Yet the *ka* was generally seen in the ancient religion as the agent for revenge against tomb intruders—which certainly fits "The Mummy Awakens."

Kameni: A Fourth Dynasty high priest of the early vulture goddess Nekhbet in her temple at al-Kab on the Nile opposite Hierakonpolis in Upper Egypt, ca. 2560 BC.

Khnum: Depicted as a man with the head of a ram, Khnum was the creator-god of Elephantine (ancient Abu at Aswan).

Punt: Hailed as "God's land" by the ancient Egyptians, Punt was probably located on the Red Sea in eastern Sudan or Ethiopia, or perhaps in northern Somalia. Egyptians apparently began traveling there during the late Fourth Dynasty (ca. 2649–2513 BC).

Qadesh: A city on the Orontes River in present-day Syria that served as a base for the Hittites against their rivals, the Egyptians, especially during the New Kingdom.

Qaqimna: The Arabic name for Kagemni, a famous Sixth Dynasty vizier. *The Teaching for Kagemni*, a Middle Kingdom text concerned mainly with the rules of gracious conduct, was putatively addressed to Kagemni. The *Teaching* itself, however, puts Kagemni in the Fourth Dynasty.

Sa'idi: An Upper Egyptian; the word for the southern part of the country—from which the Nile flows down to the North and the sea—is *al-Sa'id*, 'the elevated land.' Sa'idis are commonly seen as physically resembling the ancient Egyptians.

Zahi: Also rendered 'Sahi' or 'Djahi', in ancient Egyptian this refers to the area of roughly modern Israel, Palestine, and Syria, plus parts of Iraq on both sides of the Euphrates, in addition to Lebanon (Phoenicia) and Cyprus.

Modern Arabic Writing
from the American University in Cairo Press

Ibrahim Abdel Meguid *The Other Place* • *No One Sleeps in Alexandria*
Yahya Taher Abdullah *The Mountain of Green Tea*
Leila Abouzeid *The Last Chapter*
Salwa Bakr *The Wiles of Men*
Hoda Barakat *The Tiller of Waters*
Mourid Barghouti *I Saw Ramallah*
Mohamed El-Bisatie *Houses Behind the Trees* • *A Last Glass of Tea*
Fathy Ghanem *The Man Who Lost His Shadow*
Tawfiq al-Hakim *The Prison of Life*
Taha Hussein *A Man of Letters* • *The Sufferers* • *The Days*
Sonallah Ibrahim *Cairo: From Edge to Edge* • *Zaat* • *The Committee*
Yusuf Idris *City of Love and Ashes*
Denys Johnson-Davies *Under the Naked Sky: Short Stories from the Arab World*
Said al-Kafrawi *The Hill of Gypsies*
Edwar al-Kharrat *Rama and the Dragon*
Naguib Mahfouz *Adrift on the Nile*
Akhenaten, Dweller in Truth • *Arabian Nights and Days*
Autumn Quail • *The Beggar*
The Beginning and the End • *The Cairo Trilogy:*
Palace Walk • *Palace of Desire* • *Sugar Street*
Children of the Alley • *The Day the Leader Was Killed*
Echoes of an Autobiography • *The Harafish*
The Journey of Ibn Fattouma • *Midaq Alley* • *Miramar*
Naguib Mahfouz at Sidi Gaber • *Respected Sir* • *The Search*
The Thief and the Dogs • *The Time and the Place*
Wedding Song • *Voices from the Other World*
Ahlam Mosteghanemi *Memory in the Flesh*
Buthaina Al Nasiri *Final Night*
Abd al-Hakim Qasim *Rites of Assent*
Somaya Ramadan *Leaves of Narcissus*
Lenin El-Ramly *In Plain Arabic*
Rafik Schami *Damascus Nights*
Miral al-Tahawy *The Tent* • *Blue Aubergine*
Bahaa Taher *Love in Exile*
Fuad al-Takarli *The Long Way Back*
Latifa al-Zayyat *The Open Door*